To my cool little brother Jacob, my mom and dad, and all my friends at Epsom Primary School ~ T. B.

Thanks to change. Thanks to imagining a new life and making it possible. Thanks to all the people who were there with me, and to the ones I found on the road ~ S. S.

tiger tales
5 River Road, Suite 128, Wilton, CT 06897
Published in the United States 2020
Originally published in Great Britain 2019
by Little Tiger Press Ltd.
Text copyright © 2019 Tom Burlison
Illustrations copyright © 2019 Sara Sanchez
ISBN-13: 978-1-68010-192-8
ISBN-10: 1-68010-192-7
Printed in China
LTP/1400/2935/0919

For more insight and activities, visit us at www.tigertalesbooks.com

Imagine That!

by Tom Burlison • Illustrated by Sara Sanchez

tiger tales

It was a rainy, gray Monday morning when Elliot left 22 Green Lane to drag himself to school.

From the corner of his eye, he saw someone skipping out of the house next door.

That must be the new neighbor I saw practicing her cartwheels, he thought to himself. Why do girls always have to do cartwheels when they see a piece of grass?

"Hello!" called the girl. "I'm Ruby."

Elliot pretended not to hear her. Ruby jumped and skipped in zigzags behind him.

"What are you doing?" snapped Elliot.

"I'm trying to avoid these portal puddles, of course," beamed Ruby. "And you should, too. You never know where you might end up."

"What do you mean?" Elliot asked. "They're just puddles."

"Well, the last time I stepped in one," said Ruby, "I landed on a **PIRATE SHIP** and was held prisoner by CAPTAIN BLACKBEARD and his fierce crew. I had to scrub the **slimy** deck and polish the **PLANK** for a week!"

Elliot shook his head.

Early the next day, Ruby and Elliot met on their way to school. Elliot kicked a small pebble along the sidewalk. "That looks like a spaceship that went through the atmosphere and shrank!" announced Ruby. "I wonder what creatures were on board."

"What are you talking about? It's just a pebble," replied Elliot, walking off to class.

But later that day, Elliot couldn't help but wonder what a spaceship full of aliens might look like.

On Wednesday morning, Elliot and Ruby found a rolled up piece of paper.

"It's a treasure map!" Ruby shouted excitedly.

"Are you sure?" asked Elliot, thinking it looked more like a newspaper.

"Absolutely!" cried Ruby, holding up an old glass bottle. "And this must be what it came in."

"Imagine the adventures it has had! Who do you think threw it into the ocean?"

Elliot shrugged.

"Well," continued Ruby, "I think an **elephant** was sniffing in the **sand** when he got the **bottle** stuck in his **nostril**.

"It **tickled** him so much that he had a 255-mile-per-hour **SNEEZE**.
The **bottle** shot out of his **trunk**
and landed in the water with a . . .

SPLASH!!!"

"That's ridiculous!" said Elliot, strolling off.
"I mean, there's no way an elephant could
sneeze a bottle out of his trunk that far!"

When Elliot left his house on Thursday, Ruby was nowhere to be seen. Although the sun was shining brightly, Elliot was just thinking how dull things seemed when **WHOOPS** he almost tripped over a long, broken branch that was lying on the sidewalk in front of him.

"Hello!" giggled a voice from above. It was Ruby!
"Look at that **witch's broomstick!**" she said,
waving from the tree. "It fell out of the sky
because a flock of crows carried her to the
evil wizard!"

"Wow! But why did the crows carry her away?" questioned Elliot.

"Because she **stole** the **WIZARD'S** favorite **SPELL**," answered Ruby.

"What kind of spell did the witch take?" Elliot asked.

"It was the *Self-Replenishing Tasty Treats potion*. The evil wizard has a really **sweet tooth**, you know?" Ruby responded.

Elliot licked his lips.

Friday morning soon arrived.
"UGH!" Ruby exclaimed, scrunching up her nose. "What's that horrible, disgusting smell?"

Elliot thought for a second, and then he said, "It's probably **dinosaur dung.** Look at all those cracks along the sidewalk. The **dinosaur** must have been stomping right where we're standing! Maybe he's still **here!**"

"A **DINOSAUR!**" Ruby squeaked and threw her arms up. "Of course," said Elliot. "With **flaming red scales** and **razor-sharp teeth**!"

He looked at Ruby, and they both started laughing. Then together they raced as fast as they could, all the way to school.